REVENGE
IS A
FAMILY AFFAIR

JAKE DOHERTY

Bonus Story:

DEATH
IN A
SAFE
HARBOR

Revenge is a Family Affair

From Canada's Manitoulin Island to Ireland's County Cork

Jake Doherty

ISBN: 978-1-77242-073-9

Print Edition 2017 (Carrick Publishing)

Cover design by Françoise Doherty and Jake Doherty
Author Photo credit: Françoise Doherty

Preface

The Other Side of Despair

"Retribution leads to a cycle of reprisal, leading to counter reprisal in an exorable moment, as in Rwanda, Northern Ireland, the former Yugoslavia... The only break in that cycle, making it possible for a new beginning is forgiveness. Without forgiveness, there is no future."

~ Bishop Desmond TuTu of South Africa
Globe & Mail

Chapter One

"Fergus, wake up, it's for you."

Mary tapped him on his shoulder, but he just grunted, and tightly wrapped the hand-sewn comforter under his chin.

"It's Liam, so—"

"So it's too early, too damn that, tell him I'll call him back in the morning. Not now!"

"Yes, now!" she yelled in his right ear and pulled the covers back, almost decapitating him.

Or so it felt to Fergus. *God save me from morning people*, he thought.

"Give me the bloody phone then. Liam, it's not even sun-up here, so this better be important. Where are ya? Cork? At the paper?"

Liam didn't answer quickly, and Fergus heard only a sharp intake of breath.

"Get to it man. Your mom, is she safe?"

"Mom's okay, thank God, just a little bruising. They left her but took Conall. He's gone."

"What'ya mean gone? Gone where? Who took him? Does the Garda know?"

"Slow down Fergus. I'm not sure. Not young guys, I could tell that much. Just older guys with masks and one gun. They busted in the door when we were finishing our tea, pushed the old woman aside, grabbed him, and were gone. The coppers are dusting the place for prints."

"Gone, just like that, eh! How can I—? Keep me informed when you, well you know. Give your mom a hug for us."

By that time Mary had put on a robe, and shook her long black hair loose as Fergus explained what he had just heard. They were in the upper bedroom in their own farmhouse on Manitloulin Island, five hours northwest of Toronto and light years away from Cork, Ireland, and married only a few months, though they'd lived together for more than a year. She was Ojibwa by birth and he had come to Canada during the Vietnam War as an anti-war protester.

Which he still was, he reminded himself, the ex-Yank with an indelible mark on his soul, the way the priests had taught him. The Vietcong were bloody easy to ignore. Go to Canada instead. Easy to fit in. But not for him, not now.

"Jesus, Mary and —"

Mary sensed the cross-winds buffeting her man again, out of the north like a rogue storm. He would not go hunting like most of the men on Manitoulin, or even have a gun in the house. Or accept offers of fresh venison from friends who did hunt. On the other hand, he loved roast beef and chicken, not questioning how they arrived on his plate.

So how can I be of any use in Ireland? she wondered. *Pour everyone a drink and fly home?*

Even their few friends called them an old couple. An ex-reporter from Boston, Fergus still pretended he was writing a grand novel, and revered a tattered Bruins hockey sweater, a left-over talisman of sorts from his New England past. Mary, Dr. Mary Fraser, held art courses on the island for Ojibwa women who, like herself, had come back to Manitoulin to sort out their aboriginal identities, long-lost from childhood abuse. She was on leave from the University of Toronto where she'd received a doctorate several years earlier, and now taught art history. She detested sports clothes as juvenile.

"Took Conall, did the bloody bastards?" Fergus muttered to himself. "Should have expected this. Why him? I'm the ranking target. The ff-ing bastards. Too much Irish courage?"

First light slowly worked its way into the century-old farm house, which was still damp and cold in the way of older frame houses as they went downstairs into the kitchen. He turned on the computer, and brought up Google while she prepared coffee.

"You don't look surprised, Fergus," said Mary. "Whatever, why not, are you...?"

"Don't push me so fast woman. Give me a sec, and yes, this is worse than I expected. Bloody hell, can't those thugs accept it's over? Nobody cares 'bout the old days, not even the *Cork Times*. Perhaps the kidnapping had missed the deadline. Not a line on its website either. Strange, Liam being its editor. Why so calm? A side deal?"

Mary knew her man well enough not to push him when he was in a "mood" as he was apt to explain while working through pain and hurt, and not prepared to share. He'd been in Canada for almost 40 years since he had graduated from Boston College, and taken an over-night to Toronto instead of reporting to the US Army during the Vietnam War.

"Nothing about Conall then?" probed Mary as she handed him warmed up coffee from the micro-wave. She poured a cup for herself, and then stroked Fergus' forearm. He was almost two metres tall, and she fit under his chin, arms snuggled around his paunchy waist. This was their morning ritual on better days, as they seldom kissed.

Except in bed.

"But if you expected something like this, why didn't you tell me? Come on man, we're married, and I need to know what's under that dark soul of yours. I'm not the only one with scars and secrets. Or will you be gone in the morning, off to Ireland by yourself without a word to me?"

"Mary, that's below the belt. Don't go there."

"Okay then, Conall means a lot to you. I know that. Liam is Conall's brother, isn't he?"

He gave Mary a terse "yes", told her that Liam was Managing Editor of the Cork newspaper. Then he looked around for their Newfoundlander dog, Brinn. Fergus attached a leash to Brinn and took him into the yard for a short walk. Also a morning ritual. Mary, of course, was not satisfied with his sparse response but she knew Fergus had a dark foreboding instinct that life would always strike back at him. That goodness and peace were fleeting mirages. He, in turn, was envious that she was more practical, and preferred to deal with issues one at a time as they arose.

What Fergus didn't want to tell Mary, at least not yet, was that the Irish thugs who took Conall were no longer a small mob of aging bad guys who couldn't let go of their glorious Easter uprising in 1916, sadly followed by the execution of 14 leaders. He'd heard of the new rebellion group, who were far more lethal and active than the old Irish Republican Army, and who needed money to buy more sophisticated arms, including rockets from Eastern Europe.

The gut-wrenching truth was that he had been expecting an attack like this for some time, either in

Canada or in Ireland. Why? Going back a few years, he and Mary had been drawn into a murder near Wiarton, a small Georgian Bay town where a young Ojibwa man had been charged with the murder of an Irish immigrant who wanted to build a Casino there. Dermot Sullivan, with his brother Mick, had raised almost $7 million from IRA supporters in the Eastern United States. But peace broke out in Northern Ireland just as the brothers transferred the money from Yanks to banks in Canada. Getting drunk didn't help when Mick Sullivan ended up in a bar fight, and killed a retired Canadian General. He was convicted of manslaughter.

In time, Fergus and Mary had used their wits as citizens to find the real killer, proving that Mick Sullivan had arranged for another prisoner to kill his brother Dermot after he had been paroled.

The sticky problem was that what was left of the blood money, about $6 million, had never made it back to Ireland for the IRA. Instead, it had been seized by the FBI at the request of the Garda, Ireland's Nation Police Force. The RCMP represented the Garda and the FBI at court hearings in Toronto,

About Conall then. A childhood friend of Fergus, he had played a minor role in tracking and sorting out the money laundering but had no idea what had happened to Dermot's bank account, just that Dermot had been found in the Rankin River north of Wiarton, ON, with an arrow in his chest.

Conall had hoped the IRA, or whatever it was now being called, would park their vengeance and move on. At one time it had been the properly constituted army of the Irish Republic, only to lose most of its members who refused to swear an allegiance. Instead it became a guerilla army in the new state.

What's more, neither they nor their Yank supporters were in any position to ask for the money back. Instead, Black Irish vengeance had found new life in Eastern Europe where they bought more sophisticated arms. At that time, Libya, presumably with Gaddafi's blessings, also was a ready source.

Whatever their supplier, Fergus knew that some of the old thugs still had fire in their bellies and would kill to make a point. He realized they could be the next hostages.

Conall, wherever he was being held, was only an expendable pawn to get at Fergus.

Chapter Two

Pulling on his boots, Fergus fumbled with the laces, and reminded himself that he didn't sneak out of Boston to fight a foreign war. He was a Canadian citizen now, with a book he wanted to write. The kidnapping was, however a personal war and he knew the victim.

His wife Mary, like so many aboriginal women in their forties, was almost fully recovered from her identity crisis. Fergus remembered her black years, lost in a forensic detention centre near North Bay.

Bloody hell, he thought, *if I get involved in this mess now, could that trigger a relapse? Is it possible I might lose her again?*

Perhaps, but not likely now that she was in-his-face feisty again.

"And where do you think you are going, Fergus Fitzgerald?" She was blocking the bedroom doorway, hand on her hips. "Are you leaving me here without telling me why or where?"

Fergus' first inclination was to shrug his shoulders and give her his wide-eyed look. At least he wasn't running away, but once again he found himself stuck in the middle.

"Obviously, it's one step at a time, Fergus," she said quietly but firmly. "Call a buddy at the Ontario Provincial Police here. The OPP have helped before, and they trust you. Let Matt know this is important. At this stage, don't go to the media until we know more. Forget that you were a reporter once. Got that?"

He paused for a few seconds, recoiling. "Old reporters seldom forget anything," he replied. "If you'll clean up, I'll check the Wikipedia file about the Irish mob. I recall some earlier postings that might be helpful. Just one more thing."

"Oh?"

"Thank you for your advice. Of course, I'll not leave you behind. We're married you know."

She forced a lop-sided smile for the first time since the call came from Ireland, but sensed Fergus was not telling her the whole back story.

We need our reconciliation, she told herself. *No use asking for help from the old sources and, yes, he's awesome in the morning shower. He even lets me hold the soap sometimes.*

Two hours later

"What's so damn important, Fergus, that you couldn't tell me over the phone?" asked Matt Peltier, standing in front of a bench along the North Channel waterfront, just west of Little Current. "You and Mary ok? But make it quick, eh. I'm due in court by 11."

Staff Sergeant Peltier was Fergus' closest friend on Manitoulin, a confidant and fishing buddy. He was tall and part Ojibwa, from northern Ontario.

He sometimes intimidated Fergus. Like now, when Fergus began to stutter, hurrying his words as he tried to explain the phone call from Cork, and not anxious for a public rebuke.

"Ma…Ma…Mary's safe. At least for now. Damn, I hate that she might be put at risk!"

"Slow down, friend," said Matt, now sitting on the bench beside Fergus. "Just tell me what's happening."

Fergus stopped to take a deep breath, vainly trying to calm himself. "But the old terrorists don't take 'NO' for an answer, even if the money is locked in the US Treasury or used to buy gold or hidden in Fort Knox for all I know."

Early that evening

Matt appeared at their door with his laptop just as Fergus and Mary were cleaning up for the evening, anxious because they hadn't heard any more from Ireland. Nothing from Liam at the Cork Times or at his home.

"I'm not here," Peltier told Fergus, "nor is this laptop, OK?"

"Huh? What the—? You're telling us something about Conall then."

Matt strode past them without answering, and set up his computer on the kitchen table.

"Any coffee or tea left from supper before I explain what this is all about?"

Mary, nodded, and Fergus muttered something like "This is weird, even for a cop. Best you get on with this charade before I—"

Matt ignored Fergus for the moment, opened his computer on the kitchen table and brought up a map of County Cork near the Southern tip of Ireland.

"No questions please. Your query's gone quickly up the line really fast to Interpol, which tracks terrorism around the world. It's based in Geneva, and has links to Canada's own spooks in Ottawa. At this point, nothing is being released to the media, not in Ireland or here. So I can't explain what we know or forward the email links to you."

Fergus put his arm around Mary, looking more confused but trying to understand and accept what Matt was saying.

"So, we're supposed to look at your laptop?"

"Glad you understand. Now Mary, may I have my tea?"

The good news displayed on the laptop was that Conall was still alive, or at least had been when the computer image was taken by the kidnappers sent along to the Garda to make their point.

"Standard procedure for this sort of thing," said Matt. "If your friend had been executed, then why would anyone send money to release his corpse?"

"Point taken, I think," said Fergus. "So what's our next step? Do we just hang on until they release Conall?" He scratched his thinning hair and hugged Mary.

"Not so fast Fergus. Understand this about terrorists. These old thugs have waited a long time to get at this money, partly for more weapons, but they are also making a point that they don't want to play with the British or its Parliament. It's not just about the killing. It's the intimidation of the living. To borrow a phrase, intimidation is the gift that keeps on giving."

The three of them stood silently for a minute, until Mary shook off her doubts, and faced Matt. "My life has always been a struggle to find my place in a white world full of intimidation. Even after I was adopted by a white family in Peterborough. Now, this minute, if your computer has proof that Conall is still alive, then trust us not to impede your work or the efforts of Interpol. If

you want our help, then trust us. Show us the proof that
Conall is still alive. Or go home. Leave us!"

Chapter Three

Matt closed the computer and started to pull on his OPP jacket, but was still perplexed as to why he had come here at all. Mary's edict sunk into his cop's mind. Could he or should he trust them? Fergus had trusted him, and he was right to do so.

He's our only link to the mad Irish thugs and to their buddy, who is still being held for a hefty ransom. So what do I do, now that I'm here? Leave Fergus and Mary to look at the laptop while I take their dog for a walk?

Or let them work it out for themselves? Interpol will never know.

Back in the kitchen, what Mary and Fergus saw shocked them more than they had expected. Conall's body sagged, and had to be helped up by the masked men on either side of him. There were bruises and welts on his face and long rips in his jean legs, leaving little doubt he had been dragged into the hiding place. He was able, though, to hold his head up, but said nothing. No plea for mercy.

One of the kidnappers, the taller of the two, spoke into a microphone. "If ya want this guy back alive, and I know ya do, then find a way to get the money back from the FBI or raise it yourself. Some say $6 or 7 million was raised and later transferred to a Canadian Bank. Dermot skimmed off some for himself to build a fancy casino in Canada. That's when the cops confiscated our money. But ya knows all that, and we're giving you one week to fix it proper like. Go find his lawyer. He must have had a lawyer to look after his affairs. If Sullivan didn't put the money in a bank, then where is it now? Don't come looking for us if ya want Conall back in one piece."

"At least we know Conall is still alive," Fergus said to Mary.

She nodded, but turned away from the laptop. "Or he was when this email was drafted. Don't the police have procedures to confirm this sort of thing?"

The kitchen door opened, and Matt re-entered with Brinn.

"You are right of course," said Matt, looking for the dog's water bowl. "The Garda has procedures, but we'll start a fire in their belly if we follow that route. We have lots of other clues though. Our understanding is that our Cork mates have a good fix on where Conall is being held, probably in an old tower castle near Cork."

Fergus' spirits picked up. He'd visited Cork at least twice with Conall, and was acquainted with some of the older castles and towers, some of which dated back to the 15th Century.

"Some of these places are quite hospitable now," he explained, "and attached to more modern inns with full services. Tourists like the experience. I stayed in one when I visited with Conall and his mom. Surely they're not holding him in that one. It's much too posh to be a hideaway."

Matt nodded. "No, nothing so fancy if the Garda is right, judging by the one image. It looks far too old, with a sagging roof and hidden from the main roads. The Garda's quick research suggests it's northeast of Cork, and hasn't been inhabited for years, perhaps centuries. No known public access. Very likely that Oliver Cromwell's troops had a go at it in the 16th Century, and may have damaged it."

"Any other clues? How did they find this remote place?"

"My Garda contact said they had checked with an architect-historian, a specialist in old towers whom I met when we were both guests at a delightful summer cottage north of Peterborough several years ago. Neat guy, about 50. Just a chance meeting with after dinner drinks. I had no plans to visit Cork then, but I distinctly remember he said that a few of the older towers had been left in their original state, primarily used to shelter cattle. Almost derelict now, hidden behind heavy trees with only an unpaved overgrown path from the highway. Just faint cart tracks. Lost in time, with a dirt floor and straw for the animals.

His acquaintance had also referred to a small bit of local lore about the tower that stayed with him. "If you ever visit your friend in Cork, and want to see it, look for a small ledge on the inside wall, about three or four feet above the ground. No bottles or tools in sight but some crude weapons that were once needed to repel Cromwell's forces. The first owner and workers could have sharpened their swords and tools on those ledges. Ironical that Ireland's troubles can be traced back to Cromwell's time. The Great Protector, the British called it "troubled times" back then. Many Irish, perhaps thousands, were killed. Anyways that's what I think, that's where Conall is being held—for now."

"He'll be moved elsewhere, is that what you're telling us?"

"No, not moved," said Matt. "Take a closer look at Conall's jacket and tell me what you see."

Fergus bent over the laptop. "Just that he's gained weight. His doctor wanted him to lose a few pounds. He frets about that a lot."

"Weight is the least of his worries. Look again. This isn't body fat, it's an execution belt, packed with explosives and a detonator wired for remote firing. It could kill him like a shotgun blast of small steel balls of TNT."

The horrific image left them stunned and speechless.

Fergus looked away, breathing heavily through his hands cupped over his nose.

Mary went to the kitchen sink and began hard-scrubbing pans left from their evening meal.

Matt simply closed his computer, and quietly left.

Chapter Four

The house was still. Mary and Fergus had almost nothing to say to each other once Matt had left. They puttered around just waiting for a phone call from Liam in Cork that never came. Nor did sleep come easily in the dark, silent night.

Until Fergus needed a bathroom break, as usual, just before dawn. When he returned to bed, Mary stirred, and then suddenly bolted upright.

"I simply cannot lay here because some demented old thugs can't control their need for revenge. Damn it Fergus wake up! Oh, you are awake. Even if we had the money, I would not give it to them, so they can use it to kill more people."

"What about Conall, woman?" Fergus scowled at her, pulling a hoodie over his head. "We just let the bastards kill him, do we? A final bang, not enough left of him for a proper wake. You talk about revenge and old men, Lord Jesus, will the revenge die with them? Or must it pass onto yet another generation. At times, I think the Irish are a cursed people. Reminds me that Conall once told me we have enough religion to hate, but too often, not enough to love."

Mary found it impossible to argue with Fergus. *I'm an academic. I teach,* she reminded herself. *Dr. Mary Fraser, PhD, that's who I am. Drink only good white wine, dine at Massey College, and I'm finally holding my beautiful life together again. The successful Ojibwa, a late night television icon, ever-ready for CBC and a guide post on the reconciliation trail.*

Her arrogance, however, was too appalling even to herself. But I married Fergus in Boston, in his old University Chapel. Yes, I did, even went to a baseball game at Fenway Park where his Boston Red Sox were losing again, so I smudged him because he looked so sad. Cute though sitting in seats the Boston Irish call the Green Monster, behind some distant fence.

"Fergus, what time is it in Ireland, almost noon their time?"

He cocked his head and nodded, not looking at his watch even as he fastened it on.

"Then why can't we call Liam in Cork? He called us once. If he is busy with his paper, then leave word. At the very least, he needs to know it's impossible to raise the $6 million. Most governments are hesitant to pay ransom tax dollars to kidnappers."

"Cork Times," said a rapid-fire Irish voice, high pitched and rolling but obviously too young to be bored with life. "How may I help you?"

"Liam Fitzgerald, your editor please."

"I'm sorry sir, but Mr. Fitzgerald is not taking calls today. Terribly busy he is and all. Best call back tomorrow, or send him a note. Is this about a press release?"

"Press release? No, no, not at all. Let's just say that I appreciate his family problems."

"About his wife then? She's expecting again."

Fergus was stuck on what to say next, as it was more than obvious the Garda had imposed a tight lid on Conall's captivity and the ransom crisis without involving his professional obligations to his editorial staff and readers. Fergus' own instincts told him it was time for basic Irish charm.

He decided to take a risk. "Yes. Yes, of course, his wife Fiona had troubles with her first pregnancy, didn't she?"

"Yes, the baby pulled through, and now I have a niece. Grand isn't it? She's named Siobhan, after me."

"I understand," he said. "I married late in life so we have no children of our own. God does work in strange ways at times, my mother would say. Sainted woman she was. Tell you what, get a note to Liam to tell him his cousin is calling from Canada. I need to update him on some family matters. Can you do that for me? I know Liam wouldn't mind at all."

"Ah then," responded Siobhan slowly, "I was just figuring out you must be the Canadian cousin Liam and Fiona talk about. I'm Fiona's younger sister, and grateful for the job they found for me. If you can hold the line open, I'll ring his secretary and see if he has a minute. Back in a Dublin jiff."

No Magic Dragon

"Fergus, you've met Siobhan, Fiona's sister. Sweet child and so much like Fiona. You have news for me? My Garda sources keep me informed, but our mother just sits in the window with her friends saying the rosary. But there's no magic dragon here to pay the ransom, even if the Garda would let us."

"That's what my sources here told me," injected Fergus. "Up to Interpol and back, the FBI had solid court orders to seize the funds the Irish brothers had raised in the US. Our RCMP represented it in a Toronto court. No pot of gold to be distributed. If nothing else, the original contributors were the patsies in the money laundering scheme, and damn lucky not to be charged directly."

Liam said, however, that while he understood the FBI funds were a dead end, he wanted to pose one more question, always the curious journalist like the staff he managed at *The Times*. "Surely a wheeler-dealer like Dermot would have more than one account for little side deals. Our files show he had brought the mafia into his casino project. I realize the Casino plans died after he was murdered, but he may have advanced development funds to grease the project along. The other unknown is whether he shared any of the Yank money with his brother Mick, who was nicked for—"

"Manslaughter of an army General," added Fergus.

"Yes, correct. Brother Mick, younger of the two. He's still doing time in a prison in Eastern Ontario, south of Ottawa. I recall he was represented by a Kingston lawyer. Neat small city, great University there. Stopped there once en-route to Montreal from Toronto for more petrol and a pit stop. I cannot recall his name, the lawyer's, but our chaps here know a few reporters at a daily paper there, *The Whig Standard*, who should be able to check the paper's files for me."

Later that afternoon

"Hey, Ferg, Liam here. I'll be brief. Our curiosity about the lawyer turns out to be bang on. According to our files here, Dermot Sullivan had engaged a small law firm in Kingston, – one man shop, Emmet Costello and his wife\secretary, primarily handle only real estate and some criminal work. Nothing complicated, and not much fire in his belly. Word is from court staff that he seldom asked clients many questions. After Dermot's body was found in the Rankin River with an arrow in his chest, the local police did question Mr. Costello about the Sullivan accounts. At that point, this was still only a routine search for unusual transactions. That's not much, but at least we have a name."

Fergus was hoping for more, but tried to hide his frustration. "Routine! But thanks anyways Liam. I can only imagine how ball-breaking difficult this is for you, not being able to reach out to your own reporters. Your brother is a hostage and you can't even tell the world. Nevertheless, I had an idea this morning – that's when I get my best ideas – in the bathroom. So I'll bloody well get to the point, as my wife would tell me."

"OK, what's your point?"

"I know I'd be trusting you if I was a hostage. This is my offer. If I leave Manitoulin, I should arrive in Kingston in about five hours. Let me look after Dermot's lawyer for you. I'll find out whether he's sitting on a pile of cash undeclared from Dermot. He wouldn't be the first lawyer to use a client's cash for his own purposes. Already, Dermot's murder may be stirring police here to take a closer look at his books. If nothing else, we may be able to buy time for Conall."

Fergus was packing a small travelling bag when Mary caught up with him. She'd been into Little Current, the island's commercial centre, for some quick shopping and a visit to the local paper, *The Expositor*.

"So, you are off to Ireland, are you? When did you expect to tell me, from the Toronto airport, or one of the bars? Or a note on your pillow?"

"Nothing quite so grand, me love."

"Don't you 'me love' me, Fergus! And if you do go alone, I may not be here when you return."

"One step at a time Mary, just to Kingston."

"Kingston?"

"Of course, where else for a quick research trip for Liam, and dinner at Chez Piggy. You've always enjoyed its food."

"Do I tag along behind you taking notes?"

"Only if you insist. I would rather that you use the Queen's University Library or academic friends there to explore the psychological roots of revenge, why the Irish thugs are still chasing the old hatreds from 1916 executions after the Easter uprising, or Cromwell's bloody butchery or whatever."

"A learned dissertation then. Do we, you and Liam, have time for that?"

"Perhaps not, nor does Conall. If Liam gets a chance to talk with the thugs, then simple words may be our crucial edge between life and death. Are you coming with me woman?"

"Yes, of course. Five minutes to pack a bag then." Mary's taste in clothes was more professional then stylish, grey pant suit, smart button-down shirt and a good sweater. Unlike Fergus, she seldom used contractions in her speech, and shuddered when others did - even Fergus. Not that Fergus didn't know better. He was Jesuit-educated in Boston but given to "Bloody hell" when Mary contradicted him.

Chapter Five

Island hopping

In an hour or so, Mary and Fergus would be off the island, and onto the hard-rock shield of Ontario's Northern mainland, just past Sudbury and the darkening clouds now on the horizon, and endless chains of trucks. Mary had made ham and cheese sandwiches so there were no Tim Horton stops, just CBC radio reports about Ontario's budget problems. Time to change the radio station to easy listening music.

Whatever, just keep driving. What time is it anyway? A motel room on the water was waiting for them.

Also some place south of Sudbury, old memories about Conall came to Fergus silently without any prompting on his part.

Why Conall? he thought, mumbling under his breath.

"Fergus, you're muttering again. Speak up."

"I was just wondering, why Conall? He's the gentle soul in the family. No politics, no parades for battles lost, no—"

"No what?" Mary gently tuned in. "He was your friend. He came to our wedding in Boston. You told me he often seemed more American than Irish. But the ironic reality is that he never immigrated, and never looked for your American dream."

"None of that, please. He had a small shop on the west coast during Ireland's boom years when the British toffs liked to sail off the coast. Even, then, he made it home every night for tea with his mother. He never married and, as far as I know, was straight, too-too much Catholic for his time, with no close friends."

"None?"

"Hmm," Fergus stalled for a moment, and pulled the car to the side while he thought about the Fitzgerald tribe without Conall. "Yes, we would mourn his loss at the funeral mass, but it would be a challenge to find six volunteers to carry his casket."

Walk-up lawyer

Several hours later, finding the lawyer's office was the easy part. On Kingston Rd, E. of the city along the waterfront, it was a one-story walk-up in a building behind a gas station. The sign on the door simply read: "Emmet Costello, LLB, specializing in real estate and criminal matters."

Fergus introduced himself to an older woman, neatly dressed with rimless glasses that were held on a chain. She had three client-files on her desk, shuffling them aside as Fergus approached. A simple black-on-white name plaque identified her as "Ethel Costello", presumably Emmet's wife.

"I must first apologize for dropping in without an appointment," Fergus quickly explained, "but I'm a real estate investor now that I'm retired in Wiarton, north of Owen Sound. I saw your sign when I stopped en-route into the city proper. Very attractive area that I have been eyeing for some time. Would Mr. Costello be available for five or ten minutes? I understand how lawyers must manage their time?"

"Of course sir, Mr…Fitzgerald, I'll check."

Fergus was scanning the front page of the morning's *Whig Standard* when she returned. "I had to remind my husband that some clients are due shortly, but he would be happy to see you. This way, please."

Less than a minute passed. "Mr. Fitzgerald, from Wiarton, eh?" greeted the lawyer with well-practiced joviality for potential new clients. "Ethel and I have stopped there several times en-route to that big ferry, the Chi Chee Maun, or is it the other way around? Great future ahead and."

"Not so great as we had hoped," Fergus interjected quickly, anxious to get to his own point. "We had great hopes for a waterfront casino development that was unexpectedly cancelled when its primary investor died."

"Health problems? Heart?"

"As you well know sir, probably neither."

"Neither? What are you saying?" said Costello, now obviously flustered as he balanced forward in his leather chair. "Who are you?"

"What you need to be aware of," said Fergus, now standing with his hands on the lawyer's desk, "are these four points:

"First, you know, as I do, that Dermot Sullivan was the primary investor in the casino project.

"Second, Dermot and his brother Michael had raised the money from the IRA sympathizers in the United States, and later transferred it to a Canadian bank here in Kingston.

"Third, you were Dermot's lawyer and handled the money for him before he was found dead in a river near

Wiarton, and the money was seized by the FBI. But perhaps not all?

"Finally, my primary reason for being here is whether all this makes you an accessory after the fact. Surely you realized the Sullivans were moving dirty money around, blood money destined for terrorists, undetected money laundering to buy guns and people to be killed or maimed. With Dermot now dead, are you still holding money from Dermot's accounts for other worthy causes, or needs, perhaps, of your own?"

Costello bounded to his feet, increasingly agitated by Fergus' unexpected dissection of his problems. "I don't know who you really are, Fitzgerald, but go, just go. I'm just a small town lawyer who—"

Fergus didn't stay to hear the rest of Costello's rant, a thin denial at best. Besides it was time to call Liam and Fiona.

Liam, call first

"Make it quick Fergus. I am due for the morning meeting. Our first edition is just off the press."

Liam's blowback startled Fergus, the emphatic diction of a newsroom where time was always crucial, but seldom enough time to check the facts on every story every day. In the pre-internet world, Fergus enjoyed the rattle of typewriters at deadline when reporters literally pounded out their hurried words. Off to the press and the rush to correct the worst errors or confusing headlines. Then again, Liam had more than the daily miracle to worry about.

"Reminds me of when I had deadlines. Okay, then, on with it. Costello is a worried dude. When I mentioned that he might still be holding undeclared funds from Dermot's estate, he became very, very nervous, suddenly red-faced and sweaty. My take is that he damn well understands how vulnerable he is to legal charges, and that he may even be disbarred. That's when he told me to leave. So I did."

"Didn't deny any of what you told him?"

"He blustered a half-denial. But it was pretty transparent, and he didn't bother to threaten to sue me. That, by itself, is interesting. But that may come later, Liam. Dermot was his one big fish, and he couldn't land it. Now, he's at the bottom of the boat himself and gasping for air."

"Must go, really Ferg, staff are getting anxious. The hard fact, however, is that while the Costello melt-down would make a great page one piece someday, Conall is still a prisoner in some hovel. Can you link his abduction to Costello? Catch you later."

From Mary's cell phone to Fergus

"Must call you back, Fergus. I am in the Queen's Library stacks, very quiet as expected.

"But I have found interesting research on revenge, even Irish revenge, from a Chicago University. Give me five minutes to go outside. Miss you."

It took Fergus a few minutes to find his car and a coffee shop. He was still excited from his confrontation with Costello, but was suddenly tired from his trip from Wiarton. Black coffee with a bagel as usual. No sugar.

Just made it past the drive-through when his cell buzzed.

"Fergus here, Mary!"

"And whom did you expect, Dr. Super Sleuth?"

"Just your cool Toronto wit as always. Seriously though, did you bump into anyone you know who might be curious? Cousin Liam is almost paranoidly-cautious about security."

"Just one person, a former student from U. of T. now doing post-doctoral work in Ojibwa art. He was far more interested in a recommendation for a position here, very focused, and otherwise not interested in me. Same old, same old. Do you want me to read you my notes? Briefly put, revenge begins with children, exposed to the emotional impact of terrorism at an early age. Too young to understand; just angry that their worlds were exploding around them. That's why the impact is so inter-generational, and why Conall's captors are so old, their fears and hate kept alive by fires that never go out. When can we talk about this?"

Fergus didn't want to talk on an open line. "Mary, best if you can type your notes into your lap top, and email them to me. Must reach Liam later today. Will be in touch. And huge hugs."

"No emails Fergus, no trails. I've been burned before so I'll be brief. Okay?"

"Mary, you're an academic, and never brief, but please try. Tight and bright!"

"Well Fergus, I will try, but please remember my notes are only a synopsis of more learned synopsis about the root points of terrorism. One collective study from Loyola University in Chicago about 'Children and Terrorism' makes plain points that must first be understood. Mercifully, the writing is lucid:

"At its core, there is one central idea, that the ends justify the means. Every terrorist believes that the sacrifices made, of oneself and others, are justified by the goals and expected outcomes, whether they be secular or religious in nature.

"Also, the study says: 'terrorism includes all actions that use violence or the threat of violence against non-combatants. They use fear to manipulate people in the service of political goals.

"Most intriguing. It's a very dark view of politics, even biblical at its core. Definitely not the social justice we care about and preach. More to the point, the moral core of revenge was 'reflected in racial policies in America and South Africa', which used systematic discrimination based on race and serves as a dark aspect of each nation's history, a kind of original sin."

"Original sin, back to Adam and Eve, the serpent and the apple?"

"Think of that. If I may be allowed a personal note Fergus. Should Canada's discrimination against Aboriginal peoples be included in this list? As you might say yourself, bloody yes!

"Insight comes in many forms, even on university bulletin boards at the Library where there was a reach-out to attend a rally marking the 100th Anniversary of the Irish Revolution that began in 1916. We have discussed this before Fergus, when 14 IRA leaders were executed by the British forces in Dublin. That date, of course ignores all the troubles that preceded it by two or more centuries, like the Cromwell massacres and famines, but it does mark the beginning of self-determination, and eventually self-government for the Irish and, in time, their own country.

"Why then, has Conall been kidnapped by tired old men with their outrageous demands for monies that may not even exist anymore? The Chicago research put its primary focus on the emotional damage to children from terrorism."

"Children, Mary?"

"Yes, if this seems a stretch, Fergus, remember that the terrorists who kidnapped Conall are old men, some in their 70s or 80s, and, most importantly, are only a generation or two removed from the Easter uprising, born into homes without fathers, just laden with anger and the seeds of revenge.

"That's no different than other cultures. In time, the Irish won their independence but it's it is a victory steeped in sadness. I will share more later over the dinner you promised. But before you go, here is a thought that might be useful. Why did our thugs hide Conall in the old tower? Isolated? Yes, I get that, but it may be so isolated that any traffic would be noticed. And, most probably, it may be under surveillance already. Or did the kidnappers feel an instinctive desire to reach back in time, beyond the Easter Uprising to Cromwell's time, all yanked ahead to the present day?"

"Neatly put Mary, your sense of history reaches beyond Manitoulin!"

"Fergus, none of your blarney now. You are fishing in the wrong hole, one that's dried up!"

"No Mary! It's not that easy, it's never on the surface."

"You might be right Fergus and—damn it, my phone needs a recharge quickly. Sorry!"

"Stay with me if you can, because I must say this! The Irish laments are too old and too dispersed now on both sides of the Atlantic. Stay with your Chicago scholars, stay with their notion of original sin that stains us all. Perhaps that is what drives these old thugs. We need to see that tower through their eyes. Do they view it as their confessional for not doing more, whatever "more" is?

There was no reply from Mary.

Old friend, new source

Fergus' cell was still working well when he reached out to the *Whig Standard* newsroom and an old friend from his days at the *Toronto Telegram* where they'd both worked as young reporters. It was a wild place in those days, despite its conservative leanings. Or at least it was until taken over by the much bigger *Toronto Star*, which was Canada's largest daily and very, very liberal.

"Still working Tim?"

"Just keeping my head down really, waiting for the buy-out package, Fergie. The good ol' days are gone. But it's been a great life. Sorry I can't join you for a beer, but I have several pages to clear, mostly book reviews and columns for the Saturday edition. What about you, ever finish that books of yours?"

"Not this week anyway. Just drove my wife here to finish some research at Queen's Library. Mary's a Prof at the U of T in art history."

"Easy life, man,"

Fergus remembered that Tim always preferred life at an easy pace, good food and beer, and scotch of course, usually on pay-day as a Press Club regular.

"Why am I calling then? Some friends in Wiarton asked me to check out a Kingston lawyer who may have had some sticky fingers about a casino deal he was involved in. Out of my league, though."

"Oh, this guy got a name? We might be interested."

"Hmm. Could be a long shot though."

"Just his name will do Fergus. Might take it on myself."

"For you then, friend. Costello, Emmett Costello, small office on, give me a sec, on Kingston Road facing the water."

"Many thanks." Tim said. "*The Whig* used to pride itself on great investigative journalism. Won national awards too. But that was a long time ago. In the old days, I might be on a plane to Ireland myself."

"Ireland? Really, great pubs I know. But why now?"

"Not our story, but my wife's sister lives in County Cork, and calls frequently. Last night she chatted about a rumor that a son or brother of a newspaper editor has been held hostage by a terrorist group demanding a huge ransom. If it is true, nothing has been published yet. But it's not our story, not even our country. Poor bastards if it is true, though."

Chapter Six

Back to Mary

It was obvious to Fergus that he needed to take his car over to Queens, find the library, and hope that Mary would be waiting by the curb. All he knew now was that her cell phone was not yet fully charged. Nor was she waiting by the curb at the main entrance. Damn! Where then? Hopefully, her awesome mind would back track to a place she had mentioned when they'd last spoken. He could try the bulletin board, the one she'd mentioned, with a note about commemorating the 100th Anniversary of the Easter Uprising in Dublin. He found a handy parking space, but had no coins for the meter so he took a chance, and dashed into the Library.

"Well, that took you long enough, Fergus," said Mary, only partly in jest. "You are a very logical writer so I expected you would know where to look for me. Well done, Sherlock! Can we drive into the city now, and find a drug store for a few things I forgot when we left Manitoulin."

"Women," grumbled Fergus.

"Men! So impetuous, but useful, at times. Look near the City Hall!"

"Good, I'll find a bench near the waterfront park, and call Liam. Fine by you?"

"Of course my Lord, I too want to meet him."

"So Mary, you've worked out what we'll be doing next."

"I'm Ojibwa, I sense things. The time is right."

"I'll try to reach Liam before he goes to bed, if he's able to sleep. Must be at least mid-night in his time zone."

"Call him now then. I'll shop later."

"You're so, so right at times".

"Dial!"

And he did.

Five time zones later, Liam's home phone rang, and rang, and rang, until finally a man's loud and stern voice answered.

"No, no I told you, I'm not interested in your TV show in the morning. Not Liam, not I. Get it? I pray that you will understand."

"Understand? Yes I get that. Just as I did when Liam called me in Canada about Conall and his brother. And yes, he mentioned his mother was in near shock. If Liam's wife or daughter is about, they will vouch for me. Indulge me a minute. Who are you, guarding the phone in the middle of the night? Why should I trust you?"

"Hold please!"

"And hurry. My cell phone may lose power at any moment."

"Best say a prayer it won't, or say a prayer anyway."

"Easy for you to say, whoever you are. Tell Liam I know it's late, but it's Fergus in Canada."

"If you can spare another minute, sir, I will check with Liam's wife whom I believe is still awake. She finds reading in bed quite comforting."

Fergus had forgotten to bring a book on the trip to Kingston.

Not needed now, though. In no time he heard a woman's welcoming voice.

"Fergus, its Fiona, Liam's wife. We've met, at your first wedding near Boston. Great day it was. When Bishop Jack – he's my brother – told me about your call, we agreed to let Liam sleep as we never know what the morning will bring. These nasty old men are so hard up with revenge; I hope they blow themselves up. They're likely to kill Conall in the middle of the night, and toast each other. Or, if it's drink they guzzled, then I hope they blow themselves up, the whole lot of them."

There was a long pause and labored breathing, presumably from Fiona. "Oh Jesus, Mary and Joseph, what am I saying?" she finally continued.

"Fiona, it's obvious that you, Liam, and his mother Mona, are hurting, so I'll ring off then. Just tell Liam that I have no more news about a release. My Mary and I will be flying to Dublin either late tonight or early tomorrow. I'll let you know my flight and arrival times. Also, can you make a hotel reservation for us?"

"No, you're family and we need you here. Whatever the old mad men do, we're still a family. Bishop Jack – he's semi-retired now – and yourself included. Surely to God, as Jack himself would say, those old men must realize we cannot be intimidated by their demonic and ungodly sense of power. Perhaps they're hearing voices. If they do, it's the devil's work himself. "

Fergus said nothing from his phone in Kingston, just stared at its small case and wished he could hold his own mother, and, for a second, forget how far he was from Boston, and how close to fighting a far-off war."

"Of course we'll stay with you," he told Fiona. "I was hoping you would ask. And I know that my Mary will agree. About Liam, I don't know how I would handle the pressure as well as he seems to be doing. On the brighter side, he has you to come home to, a good and strong woman at his side."

"Well thank you of course, but truth be known, how he deals with my red-headed temper is a blooming miracle sometimes."

"Not to worry, at least about Mary and myself. She'll enjoy meeting you. As you know, I lived alone for several years after my first wife died from cancer when she was very young. She was a teacher from Newfoundland, and brightened my life. Now, my new wife Mary is aboriginal and, well, she doesn't talk about this much now, but has had to overcome some very dark years."

"And, bless her, did she overcome that?"

"Yes, in time, she had been abused as a child on the reserve and then, in her 40s, had a serious identity crisis after she had watched a killing but couldn't stop it. She was even charged with murder and ended up in a forensic detention centre, but was released when a teenager later confessed."

"Is she strong now?" Fiona asked.

"Very! Then again you can judge for yourself tomorrow. Liam has my number and we'll be up about noon your time."

Chapter Seven

Beyond the famine

Fergus and Mary stayed overnight at an airport hotel. They took a flight via Dublin to Cork and then onto the Fitzgerald home where Fiona and Mona were waiting, high on a hill overlooking Cork City and the River Lee. Like the neighboring houses, more comfortable than pretentious. A high school was nearby, with separate buildings, of course, for the girls and boys. Quite proper and accessible for an editor's family – easy to find for Canadian visitors, and, tragically, for kidnappers who had taken Conall away and brutalized him, forcing him to wear a suicide vest.

The Cork kidnapping was an anomaly. As Fergus recalled from previous visits, Cork had become a prosperous city of about 126,000 residents. And enviously safe with police cars seldom evident on the bustling main streets along the River Lee and beyond. No British soldiers now, like the infamous Black and Tans. Even England's Queen Elizabeth came once in May 2011, not quite asking to forgive and forget the centuries of repression, but more of recognition that Ireland is its own sovereign nation now, with open and free elections. The Irish, being Irish as Fergus would say of course, threw her a sumptuous state dinner in a Dublin Castle. Prince Phillip came along, as usual.

Not that everyone in Ireland was prosperous at that time, nor had the relatively small country put aside all of its troubles. So many financial institutions and individuals were hard hit by the global recession that began in 2008. The collapse of the Irish Stock Exchange became known as the St. Patrick's Day Massacre. Seniors also lost their health cards and more taxes were added.

Why are many Irish so gracious now, to visiting tourists, even visiting writers? Consider a lesson about the famine by Tim Pat Coogan, well considered as Ireland's best known historical writer: "Psychiatrists with knowledge of Irish history trace it back to the condition of 'learned helplessness' from the famine years..."

Indeed, by contrast, Northern Ireland has remained, in effect, a province of England but there are virtually no inspections at border crossings now. Only one sign reminded tourists that while Ireland trades in Euros as befits its membership in the European Union, Northern Ireland uses pounds like the United Kingdom bastions of England and Scotland.

Fergus even liked telling strangers that he was visiting from Canada, relishing the instant and welcoming banter. "From Canada, are ye, so how can I help?" Many Canadian visitors, particularly from New Brunswick, feel very much at home here, almost sublimely comparing Cork to Saint John, NB and its working harbor, fed by a long river from the north of Saint John. Much of its early growth came from the first wave of United Empire Loyalists fleeing the American Revolution in 1776 and its inclusive sense of democracy. The Loyalists dominated politics and commerce for the next two centuries,

The first Irish settlers came in the 1830s, but the most crucial divide came in the 1840s during the potato famine in Ireland, when many British lords and landlords shipped their crops to England as usual, ignoring the famine in the fields. Many peasants left for Canada, but many died on typhoid-infested ships or on quarantine islands in the St. Lawrence River.

Chapter Eight

Rumors catch hold

Tea, of course was also waiting, a ritual for the Fitzgerald family, but no news about Conall. "Liam's not for telling about Conall over the phone," said Fiona. "We've been really careful since you warned us about rumors making their way to Canada. Even if we were approached, we wouldn't confirm or deny the rumor. What do we do now?"

Another voice answered quickly and firmly. Impatient really.

Liam strode into the room, ready for action.

"We can bloody well ask the Garda where they suspect he's being held, can't we?" he said. He spread out a map of Munster Province, the largest province in Ireland at the southeast corner of the country. "And for heaven's sake, you two," he said to Fiona and his Mom, "give them coffee or something stronger; they're from Canada you know."

Liam was an inch or so taller than his cousin Fergus, and only his tie and collar were undone, vest buttoned, and coat now hung on the back of a chair – the work-a-day dress code for editors who must dance between the newsroom and the publisher's office. He was in his early fifties.

"I can only stay a few minutes. Just as I was preparing to leave the office, Seamus, my Garda keeper, arrived in his civvies, not wanting to attract attention as an inspector. But with Fergus here and Dr. Mary as well, and Fiona too, and our mother Mona, he understood my rush to get home."

"You've brought news about Conall, have you?" asked Fiona. "I was just baking a few things for our guests. So get to it Liam, have we beaten the bastards, if you don't mind my language Dr. Mary. Not what you're probably used to, being a professor and all."

"Please, don't mind me," said Dr. Mary, taking a tea cup from Mona.

"Not much to pass along I'm afraid, at this point," said Liam. "But Seamus did tell me the Garda search time has narrowed down where Conall might be held hostage. The site is unconfirmed, but their over-flights have noticed unusual traffic in and out of an old tower northeast of Cork, in the rolling hills of the Neglas Mountains, most likely derelict now, and hidden by an encroaching forest."

"Any license plates available," asked Fergus, shaking off the drowsiness of the long flight from Canada, "in or out?"

"Not that the Garda can make out," replied Seamus, standing now, and preparing to leave. "Assuming this is the right place, the vehicle shifts would be made at night, and, perhaps not every night. Nor can we leave a cruiser or an unmarked vehicle posted on the road where the cart tracks end."

Liam stood and reached for his suit coat, taking a scone for the road. "Must go back for a few hours, tackling more paper work as always. I assume Fergus and his Mary have seen the Interpol emailed video of Conall that Sean asked be made available to you."

Fergus and Mary both nodded they had seen it, with its unforgettable image of Conall, beaten and bloody, wrapped in an execution vest, the hostage-takers ready to kill him instantly if would-be rescuers blundered in.

"Whatever we do next, we must deal with the terrorists first," said Liam, taking his leave of the group.

Walking toward his car, Liam thought, *If Conall were to be killed, would the crazies come after Fergus next, here in my home? More bloodshed, more revenge?*

If in doubt, go for a walk

For several moments, no one in the room commented on Liam's last remark, until Dr. Mary put a hand on Fergus' leg and said, "I hope you don't mind if I take my man here for a walk down to the river. It's been such a rush just getting here that we need to breathe your fine Cork air with its tinge of salt, and stretch our legs. Can you show us on a street map where we are, and point us toward the school and beyond to the River Lee?"

Fiona gave them a street map with advice that they should not tell anyone where they were staying. She suggested that, if asked, they should give the name of a local hotel, and say they were Yanks on a honeymoon. Lots of folks in Cork had Yank and Canadian relatives, so they wouldn't stand out too much. Just newly-weds.

They ambled past the school yard where youngsters were playing innocently. A middle-aged teacher sitting on the school steps waved them over, and asked whether they had children of their own. Both blushed a little, explaining they had married late in life. Without giving the teacher her name, Mary knew she had to tell the teacher about life on a reserve, with a hint about smudging, if she expected the teacher to respond in kind. Even with her doctorate and academic position at one of Canada's most respected universities, Mary accepted in her own way that she was a stranger again in a white world, not an enemy to be feared, just different and not easily trusted. At times, the unfairness of the imbalance irked her, the unspoken and unthinking hint of distrust.

Get over it, she told herself. *No one will abuse me as my father had. I'm not a victim, anymore.*

"Your children have so much energy," said Mary. "No fighting, just playing well together."

The teacher nodded. "And yours?"

"I teach art history at the University of Toronto now, but I grew up on an aboriginal reserve in Northern Ontario, Canada where life was often abusive. But I am still very attached to the Ojibwa First Nation."

The teacher chose to remain positive, and simply touched Mary's arm, not wanting to probe the dark side of aboriginal life with a stranger. "I'm intrigued by your tribal experience. But duty calls and, regrettably, I must return the children to their classrooms. Too haunted we are, most of the day."

"Haunted by whom?" Mary jumped in. "Are there ghosts here, or—?"

The teacher grinned. "Whoa, as we say in Cork. Ghosts! Nothing supernatural intended. Just that I feel lucky and fortunate to be here, at this time, for the children, so much future ahead."

Mary decided not to press the point. "Yes, of course, time is so precious. If we had more time, I would tell you about smudging, a ceremonial blessing with herbal smoke, that really brought my husband and I together. He even sent me a love letter."

The teacher turned to make one last comment as the school bell rang the end of recess.

"Smudging and a love letter, eh? Not very Irish, but oh how we could use them here. We have a long and deep history also. And of course we have had our independence for years, but still, desire for revenge and the animosities keep burning. It's not even in our newspaper yet but there are rumors a young man has been held hostage by some old men, some say maybe terrorists. The Times is a great paper that I read every day, but I'm bewildered now by its silence. Pray God the rumor is just gossip, stirring up more revenge. Must go inside now so safe journey home. Canadians, 'eh'! That much I know from a relative in Kingston."

And with that, the teacher was gone.

Chapter Nine

Bishop Jack joins the hunt

With dishes cleared away, Mary plopped down on a comfortable sofa beside Bishop Jack. Judging by his dinner table chatter, she sensed he was intrigued about her chance meeting with a local school teacher, and her concerns about *The Times'* cone of silence.

"Bishop Jack, may I call you that?"

"Oh no, just Jack please in this house, Mary. I'm retired now and prefer sweaters and slacks to cassocks. It is clear, though, that you wish to ask me a question. I shall be flattered if you do."

"Indeed. I'll try to be brief. But if I'm treading into places where you will be uncomfortable, just tell me as we go along. If nothing else, I am a guest here in a culture that isn't mine, charming and hospitable though it is."

"My dear Mary, I did a lot of parish work before I became bishop, not that I could reveal what I heard in the confessional, even when I was a curate. So, let's get to the fact of the matter."

"I understand. I need to know more about the awful men who kidnapped Conall and their desperate sense of revenge. My Fergus heard much the same rumor in Canada before we left for Ireland. A woman in Cork has a relative in Canada, and passed along the same story through a Canadian reporter. Unfortunately, his paper wasn't interested. Still, it could be the same rumor from a second source, could it not?"

"Neatly put indeed! And?"

Before he could answer, Liam's mother was standing in front of them, obviously curious about their tete-a-tete on the sofa, but much too polite to intervene. Apron still on and tea-pot in hand, Mona took the gracious route, offering them more tea.

"Just a few drops left in the pot, can I...I mean, may I top up your cups? No trouble at all Jack, just trying to help out."

"Sit with us a bit," said Jack. "Good woman that you are with your own circle of friends, I suspect you know more people around here than I do, and certainly more than Mary does."

Mary though, sensed that Mona needed to be helped more gently to reach beyond her comfort zone. "Your turn then Jack."

"Just this then. Mary and I agree that, theoretically for now, we have two possible leads about rumors that your Conall has been kidnapped. We don't know whether that's idle talk or malicious gossip. Who knows whether one of the kidnappers has leaked where they are holding Conall? If so, why then? Can their unholy need for revenge burn out before Conall dies, or before the Garda can rescue him? If Conall dies, do they not realize that the courts will not be lenient with them? Our judges and public prosecutors will come down hard on them. Whatever the reason, we must ask ourselves whether that's significant. Perhaps. Without bothering Liam and Fiona at this point, may I propose that you and I join our curiosities and concerns about poor Conall, and trace the rumors as best we can?"

Mary was pleased, and smiled for the first time that evening.

"Jack, I sense that you are close to the same age as Fergus and I. We think the terrorists are, in their 70s or 80s, closer to Liam's mother's age. And with your sense of place in Cork and its people, you must have heard a lot of gossip in your rounds and, perhaps, probed a little."

"Well, I never hit anyone with my crosier. If I may be irreverent for a moment, it's just a stick with a cross on its top. Like most bishops, I do know how to be persuasive when the need is a matter of life and death, as is most certainly the case here. In good conscience, can we stand by and not help Liam, his blessed mother and Fergus to rescue Conall? So, Mary, how can I help?"

"Start with the teacher I met at the school near here. When and how did she hear the rumor? I'll try not to get her principal curious and involved. Perhaps you know them already. The school is so near this home."

"And you, where do you fit in? Or do you wait until you return to Canada?"

Mary paused in reflection, hands closed in front of her face, almost in silent prayer. "I shall tell Fergus, of course, as he first heard about the Canadian rumors from an old friend in Kingston. All I want from him is the name of the woman who has a relative in Ireland. I hope that the rumor trail in Canada is not too long. Anyway, our country is very large; however it is measured, east to west, and way north to the arctic, but the internet helps to close the gaps. If successful, I'll visit the Irish relative here, and ask how she heard the rumor."

Background in bed

"Fergus don't go to sleep on me. I need you…well, not that way, perhaps later. Just listen to what Jack, Bishop Jack to you, and I are proposing."

"Oh my God, has the bishop proposed to you? I saw him chatting you up. But he's too old for you, and he's a celibate priest and you're not."

Mary had to restrain herself from waking the whole house. "Fergus, you can be so damnably clever at times. No, no, no, not that kind of proposition, clunk head. We all have common cause to save Conall, presuming that he is still alive. I asked Bishop Jack to question the school teacher we met yesterday on our walk. Remember her? Good, I can proceed then. And she also said she had heard a rumor that Conall had been kidnapped. Also, she was very concerned that Liam's paper had not published the smallest of stories about it. At my request, he will try to see her for more information, a name perhaps, of who told her and that sort of thing."

"Really? You and Jack, as you call him, have agreed to work this case?"

"In the morning, or at the noon break for the teacher probably."

"Makes bloody good sense. So, Mary, what's your role? Take out a classified perhaps, go on line?"

"No, no," she grinned. "Get serious, man. Can you backtrack to your *Whig* buddy in Kingston? Can you get the names of the two sisters, particularly the Irish relative who first reported a possible leak? We need to know who, and, more importantly, why someone has gone public. By accident or, perhaps more strategically, to rattle Liam and Siobhan or the Garda."

Fergus called Canada

"Tim, I need your help again."

"Fergus, hey guy, you just reached me before I head home. And I owe ya. Your tip on the lawyer with sticky hands is paying off. Front page even. So what's up now?"

"A lot, a good friend of mine here has been kidnapped by some old guys left over from the Irish troubles, part big-time extortion and very big time revenge."

"I thought the troubles had passed. The republic has its own independent government, that sort of thing."

"Not quite," said Fergus. "Revenge never seems to die. The mad men who took Liam's brother Conall, are in their 70's or 80's but have threatened to kill Conall and…Well that's why we need your help."

"Write a piece for the Saturday feature page?"

"Later I can help you with that. Right now, can you give me the name of your wife's friend or relative in Cork, the one who heard rumors about the kidnapping of the brother of *The Cork Times'* editor? The *Times* can't expose the plot, or even tell its own staff. My Mary is searching for the name of a teacher who also has heard the rumor."

"Same rumor?"

"Perhaps. But we need to back track the rumors, and get a firm lead where Conall is being held. All I want from your sister is the name of the person who told her about it. We don't know if the old guys are deliberately yanking our chain, or just getting sloppy about whom they tell."

Tim went quiet for a few seconds, asking himself whether he should involve his sister and, perhaps, put her at risk.

"Okay, Fergus, if this works out for you, don't mention where you got your information. It's still not my war, but do you have a laptop with you? And, if we send you a name, don't bother to confirm receipt by email. Instead call me at home in a couple of hours. We'll talk soon."

In no time, Fergus received a short email from Tim, with a name.

> *Bridget McCarthy is my wife's relative. She lives in Kingston, is a mother of eight, a widow who spends most evenings chatting with relatives. She telephones often with a teacher in Cork, and also another friend here in Canada. Bridget is not believed to be particularly political though. She's the one who called in the kidnapping rumor.*

Morning coffee break

"Oh, her," said Mona, insisting that everyone had matching teacups. "I can call Bridget if you like – we're old friends, wouldn't you know. She moved to Canada after her husband died, from the cancer. You finish your coffee, and I'll use the phone upstairs in Liam's office."

In no time at all, she rejoined the group, reporting that Bridget's late husband, Gabriel, had known about the kidnapping, and had wanted desperately to go along with his older buddies one last time. He had even forgotten to bring his meds the day of a planning meeting. In the end, he asked Bridget and his family to forgive him for his weakness.

No doubt, it was through Bridget that the Kingston leak occurred. Gabriel had been an old man who carried an equally old desire for revenge with him to his grave.

"And, oh, I almost forgot," Mona added, "Bridget's relative in Cork is Ann Marie who teaches at the big Catholic school here down the road. You folks probably met her yesterday. A good woman, but why is she so angry at Liam's paper with Conall's life at risk?"

Chapter Ten

From the shadows

Fergus and Mary found Ann Marie that morning coming out of her classroom. At first she was only moderately surprised to meet them again, tightly controlled in her attitude, but she broke into tears when they told her what they were about, and asked for her help.

At first, Ann Marie just looked away, head down.

Not to be deterred, they told her they had been talking to Bridget in Kingston, and described Bridget's grief over her late husband's almost deadly fascination with the kidnapping.

"No, no. I can't talk anymore. Sweet Jesus, I can't put my husband at risk. He knows too much now and—"

Stepping out from a shadow along the school wall, Bishop Jack came forward as planned. He had volunteered to help if needed, and spoke softly now, leaning more than usual on his cane. His knees were usually quite painful from the encroaching arthritis, but not at this moment.

"We've known each other a long time, Ann Marie," he said, "in good and bad times. I know you have nothing to confess, but it's time to do something good."

"Why? My man, he's done nothing wrong," she replied, removing a tissue from her small leather purse, the kind of handbag women of her generation always carried. When the sniffling was under control, she stood straighter, all five feet of her. "I swear, he just had a few beers with old friends of his father, and was asked to join, be one of them, be a real Cork man like his da. Told me all about it, he did. It's our money, he told me, and they wanted it back, wanted to make the English and Yanks respect us."

"Was he prepared to kill one of our own, Conall, a good and decent man?"

"Kill Conall? Of course not. Rubbish! Didn't even know who the thugs might be. He said 'no' and came home terribly torn about remaining silent."

Bishop Jack, Mary and Fergus, looked at each other with eyebrows arched, wanting to believe Ann Marie but not quite prepared to.

Fergus looked away, one hand over his eyes. "We're all on trial here," he told them. "Give in now to the dark side, and what's left, more distrust, more hate? Pardon me Jack for being blunt, but it's clearly time to believe Ann Marie as the good woman she is, trying to hold her family together."

Fergus put his arm around Mary to steady himself before going on. "I left my family in Boston once because I could see no good in going to Vietnam with our guns and coffins. More than 58,000 Yanks killed there," he said in a lower voice. Then suddenly rising defiantly, he added, "For what? Now I have my Mary. We really despised each other when we first met back in Canada, quick to criticize, and run away from old wounds. Without making this sound like a silly, cure-all soap opera, we began to realize that we preferred asking questions, and sharing our cultures more than walking away and playing the blame game!"

Mary wiped away a tear, reached over, and kissed him on the cheek, and Jack hugged them both, very un-bishop-like, but much needed.

"Let me ask Ann Marie the central question," said Jack, standing tall with his renewed sense of purpose, more priestly than posh. "I accept the decision your husband made. We can help him with the Garda. In turn, can he offer any hint as to where Conall is being held?"

With her free period almost over, Ann Marie began to edge back into school, head down.

Jack held his ground, both hands on his cane, not to be denied by her reluctance. "He said nothing then?"

"Well nothing specific, just it was an old derelict tower north of Cork. There are lots of them in the Nagles Mountains, at least an hour's drive away. Not even on a real road. Hope this helps a tiche, but I must go now. Sorry, that's all I can remember."

As Ann Marie re-entered the school, Jack and Fergus raised their eyebrows, more out of curiosity than excitement.

"Well, well now," said the bishop. "Shall I call Liam with this tidbit, and let him decide whether to pass it along to the Garda?"

"Of course. At last we have a hint. Irish luck perhaps but before—"

"Before what Fergus? What's bothering you?"

"Just double checking. Habit I guess, the old reporter in me. A habit that's served me well. Before we point at the Nagles Mountains, what do we really know? Are they really mountains?"

"Fair question Fergus. Of course the Nagles, strictly speaking, are not mountains like the Alps, or your towering Rockies. They're just hills, really, and I recall some being reforested. Most of the roads are quite rough."

"Derelict are they? Not in use then."

"Only sporadically," replied Jack. "I'm told some of our young curates use them for mountain biking. The place is crisscrossed with trails. Definitely not my cup of tea."

Mary edged in between them to make her point. "It's time, gentlemen, to call Liam. From what you said Jack, and I agree, Ann Marie's courage deserves a proper hearing. She trusted us, and the least we can do is honor that. So back up the hill to the house and find the number of Liam's private line."

Jack, always the prudent shepherd, didn't want to move as quickly. He stared down at his well-polished black shoes. "And if Liam does not answer, do we wait?"

Fergus scowled at him. "Wait? Bloody hell no! If you can excuse my anxiety, I can't forget the picture of Conall our local police shared with us before we came. He'd been badly beaten with a bomb wrapped around him that could blow him apart in seconds. Yes seconds."

He reached over to the bishop, and slowly drew a cross with his thumb on Jack's forehead. "Trust me Jack, good editors can always be reached. They understand when time is precious and seconds count."

And up the hill they went

"Mr. Fitzgerald, ah Fergus, Liam has your note and will call you within five minutes."

"Why the delay, Siobhan? Did you tell him it was urgent?"

"It's just that, well, don't tell him I told you, but he's waiting for the Garda man who will listen in. Very Cork, right brilliant times ahead."

"Listen in? What is this, a party line? Next you'll be telling me his mother wants to listen in as well. Of course, I'll wait."

Wait for what, wondered Liam's mother, Mona, sitting at home quietly off to the side. She didn't say much anymore, but worried about her country's future, breeding more children who carried scars that could last a lifetime. *My own father, bless him, told us about the days when the British burned Cork.*

"You are crying now, mother Mona," said Bishop Jack sitting on a hassock in front of her. "Just hold my hand. Liam will be here soon, and we'll tell him our news about Conall. And you have spilled your tea, so let me get more."

"No more tea, thanks, just tell me if you will, what year was it when Cork burned?"

"When Cork burned? Almost a hundred years ago, yes, yes, before our time, about 1920. Hundreds homeless and thousands jobless. Your father's time perhaps. Did he ever speak about that?"

"I can still hear his voice but not what he said. It's in me like some stain on my soul that I can't rub off. But didn't some bishop threaten our people? Oh Lord, don't let me remember any more. Just help my Conall."

Chapter Eleven

Where's Conall?

Very much a modern and confident young woman, Siobhan was not quite chirpy as usual. She put one arm around Bishop Jack's shoulder and the other gently clasped her grandmother's hands.

"Liam is here, parking in the garage as usual. He's following the Garda's advice to stay with his normal routine. Oh, at last, here he is."

Liam nodded to his sister-in-law and went quickly to the centre of the room.

"You all have met Seamus, from the Garda who will bring us up to date. Progress is being made. Seamus, meet the family." The officer, not in uniform, moved crisply beside Liam, speaking without notes.

"Let me get to the good news. My colleagues are certain that Conall, as expected, is being held in an old tower in the Nagles Mountains."

Fiona interjected, not wanting to embarrass her husband. "We agree that's where Conall is being held in the mountains by those nasty old men. At least that's what our sources have been telling us."

"Your sources?" Liam asked.

Before his wife could explain further, his mother bolted between them. "God doesn't care about sources, Liam. Why isn't Conall with you? Have you forgotten him some place? Mother of God, I thought I saw him coming through the door with you, with his lop-sided grin and…straight here, yes, yes, straight here from school. Or did he get lost again? Bishop, can you find—?"

Seamus stepped forward and took off his jacket, placing it neatly on a chair. He loosened his tie.

Bishop Jack understood the 'disrobing' gesture, having spent most of his life amid rituals and uniforms of a different kind. Change his image; change his freedom to speak freely. Seamus was not a member of the family, but he was closer to them now than he had been while wearing his suit jacket.

"Mother Mona," Seamus said gently, "when you say your prayers tonight, know that Conall is on a high mountain top. Liam will be with him soon to bring him home. And please Mother Mona, there will be time later to tell your friends."

Seamus looked around at the family, making sure they each had taken his point. Mona was clearly suffering from dementia, and could not be trusted to keep their plans quiet.

Liam nodded his understanding, accepting that this was an inevitable moment. He had sensed his mother's confusion for the past several weeks. He knew she was moving in that misty grey space, sometimes out of touch, but, mercifully, sometimes more lucid again.

He'd seen it happen in his newsroom, when an older colleague would show the first signs of dementia under complex newsroom pressures, and just walk away until his head cleared. Or, over time, sink into the long black night of Alzheimer's. He knew the journalist could eventually be replaced, but as a father, a grandfather, it was a different story. His family could not replace their loved one so easily.

Nor could Liam replace his mother.

Damn those thugs who took Conall, Liam thought. *Should we show mercy when we find them? Or, were they also childhood victims of terror and revenge themselves?*

At least their old age means their children would be middle aged now and not so vulnerable. If we let the old bastards walk away, would the old wounds and hatreds eventually burn off like a morning fog over the harbor? Or would there be more killings if we let them keep their hatreds burning?

No, our first priority is to rescue Conall. Save one soul at a time. But can we reach him in time? Yes, yes that's the issue. Perhaps we don't need more journalists or editors, just exorcists and their incantations.

Chapter Twelve

Leg or breast?

Mona was exhausted. The group decided to move their meeting from Liam's office to their home.

With Mona settled in her bed, they sat in the parlour, pouring tea.

Before Seamus could resume his update, they heard a sudden screech of brakes, the squeal of tires, followed by muffled chatter and halting footsteps up the walk toward the house. Someone was pounding on the door.

Fergus ran to the window – but was too late.

The home's front door crashed open and a headless chicken was tossed inside with a note tied to its wing.

As Fiona screamed, the Garda officer pulled out his cell phone and called his headquarters in Lower Cork, not far from the western shore of the Lee River.

"We are under assault here and need protection."

"Protection! We are alerting all cars in area as I speak, sir! Whoever did this won't get far. Any gun fire, sir?"

"Gun fire? Hell no, just a headless chicken."

"Oh, right on it sir. Would there be finger prints on the chicken, sir?"

"Get serious man."

"Trying to sir. May I suggest that the chicken be covered as is, and returned by car to Headquarters for examination? It's possible sir, that one or more of the group behind the intrusion may already be known to us. If so, can you find a secure place for this chicken, and the note of course?"

"Consider the bird duly bagged, Constable," Seamus said, his eyes twinkling.

"May I suggest two bags sir, one for the chicken, and the other, of course, for the note. It can be difficult to read finger prints through chicken grease or blood, sir."

"Very fast work indeed, Constable. Must go now, as one of our cars has just pulled up in front of the house. Well done, young man. Oh, just one more thing."

"Of course, sir. What particular 'one more thing' were you thinking of?"

"Complete secrecy, Constable. This case is still very hush, hush, and no nibbling at the evidence, both the chicken and the note of course." Seamus knew there was a comic element to the story, and it would be tempting for the young Constable to share it with his mates.

"Of course sir. What did the note say?"

"Yer running out of time. Where's the money?"

"Ransom?" said the constable. "Don't we have a policy against paying out, sir?"

"Not my call, Constable. Ah, we'll get back to you, with the chicken note, of course."

"Right sir."

For a long moment, no one in the parlour knew quite what to say. The chicken, of course, was bagged and tagged as evidence, and Liam and Fergus went looking for the half-full bottle of Irish whiskey. Bishop Jack joined them as well.

Seamus declined the offer of a drink as, technically, he was still on duty.

With a nod from Liam, Seamus took his place again in the centre of the room.

"First off, regardless of what happens to the chicken," he said, "the strategic question has become more certain. Are we running out of time to save Conall? Even if you had the ransom funds, which I presume you do not, the Garda and the government advise not to pay."

"And why not?" thundered Bishop Jack, waving his cane. "Conall's life is sacred to everyone here. Are you recommending we condone murder if this wretched situation comes down to that?"

Mary took her hand away from Fergus, and put her arm around Jack. In many ways, she had been living her life as an academic, and she knew when not to rush into rash decisions. Instead, if tobacco had been handy, Mary would have reached back into her Ojibwa heritage and smudged everyone in the room, and would have suggested that her new family, Jack, Liam, Fergus, and Fiona, all breathe deeply. She would teach them to trust in their own sense of goodness.

Liam stepped into the family circle.

"Let me make this clear, I am not recommending paying ransom. And forget about that blessed chicken. If anything, all it means is that the kidnappers are becoming desperate, using cheap theatrics to make a point. That kind of crap – my staff at the paper have to sort threats out like that every day.

"What Seamus and I can now tell you is that the Garda has been sending flights of planes over possible sites, now focusing on the old towers in the Nagles, particularly those that are well beyond the main roads. They believe they know which old tower is being used."

"I appreciate that the Garda know what they are doing," interjected Bishop Jack, "but I must ask, are they sure? Are they still searching several old towers, or just this one?"

Ever the policeman, Seamus gathered his thoughts before speaking. "It's just too cruel not to help your mother and just walk out the door," he told Liam. "I don't want to five Mona false hope. Agree?"

Liam nodded.

Turning to the family, Seamus said, "Now Liam and I must leave for a few hours."

A walk in the woods

With the chicken crisis behind them, Liam and Seamus said their good-byes, and left for their offices and every-day responsibilities.

"Before you go," said Liam waving Seamus into his car, "my sense, from what I heard today, is the Garda will be attacking the old tower in the Nagle woods very, very soon. As I have promised, I have spoken only to my family, and there have been no leaks to or from my newsroom, nor will there be any until the rescue team finishes its work. I have kept my word."

"You have indeed, Liam, or I wouldn't be talking to you now, no doubt with your family peeking through the curtains. Yes, you have kept your word, and I believe, so has your family. What then?"

"I realize that I am neither trained, nor authorized, to join the Garda assault squad and, hopefully, the rescue team. Even if I've had nightmares about what could happen, leading the charge into the old tower, and saving my brother, it's what older brothers do in a crisis."

"I understand completely, Liam. I'd want to join the rescue too, if I were in your shoes. But I sense you want something else."

"I assume an ambulance will follow your officers, staying in the shadows while they bust in to rescue Conall. That is, if they can save my brother in time before his captors blow him up. Oh God, I can still see how bloody awful he looked in that email they sent us to make their point. Only one outcome seemed possible then, Conall more dead than alive. And I would need to tell the final outcome to my mother myself. Whatever the outcome, before I become the editor again, and talk to my news room, I must be the good son and good brother first. May I ride in the ambulance?"

Seamus sucked in his breath, and said nothing for a few moments, impressed by Liam's sense of duty to his blood kin in the Fitzgerald tribe. "I shall take this to my superiors and get back to you promptly. Do you have a black track suit with a hoodie?"

Several hours later at home

"Back to the office Liam? It's getting late."

"No, Fiona. Just shopping for a workout kit, and what's it called, a hoodie."

"Really! You already have a green hoodie. Won't that do?"

"Ah, perhaps, but I think I look better in black. I'll be back soon."

Note for Fergus

Liam's wife and mother exchanged worried glances, hesitant to challenge his cover story. *Black hoodie indeed! Besides he never has time to work out even though he is starting to develop a paunch.*

He is a thoughtful son, Fiona mused. Running to a front window to catch one last look at her husband, she also noticed a piece of *Times* stationary on a side table in the entrance hall. It was addressed to Mother Mona and herself, no address or stamps:

Just one sheet of his paper, addressed to them both.

> *No time to explain before I left but I have arranged to travel with the ambulance crew to the hostage site. The Garda approves. As soon as I know the results, I will phone you. I will stay with Conall when the ambulance folks take him to a hospital for examination. Bishop Jack knows all of this.*

Dr. Mary looked at the family members, unable as an outsider to read their faces. She noted that Fergus also held his silence, keeping his head down.

"Damn you Fergus," she muttered under her breath. Bishop Jack returned her worried look, but said nothing.

"I am not a blood member of this family" added Mary "so please, help me understand what is happening at this moment?" Giving in to her frustration with their do-nothing demeanor, she added, "In my old world as an

Ojibwa, someone would offer to make more tea, or whatever. May I?"

Bishop Jack was the first to reply. "Of course, good doctor, tea it is."

And so tea it was as the Fiona's sister Siobhan jumped up first to put the kettle on, and then Mary passed around the cups gently, holding each person's hand as she did.

Fergus, without explanation, withdrew from the family circle and rushed upstairs to his room.

A few minutes later, much to everyone's amazement, Fergus returned pulling on his black raincoat, and then his black toque. "No time to explain, Liam's waiting's for me."

Mary was furious. "And where do you think you are going, mountain man?"

"Later, later," he replied gulping air as he pushed past her. "Must catch up with Liam. Fiona, where do you keep your axe?"

"Axe?"

"Yes. An axe! With a sharp cutting edge and a long handle. For chopping wood."

Fiona replied, "I don't remember where it is."

The door suddenly few open. Liam's son John Patrick had come home unexpectedly, hoping to surprise his family. Unfortunately he'd just missed his father who had left to join an ambulance team following the Garda rescue squad.

JP was about two inches taller than his father, and much lighter. He lived just off campus sharing the cooking with two mates, one from near Cork, and the other from Donegal.

"So where's the old man?"

His mother looked speechless, not knowing how to explain where Liam and Conall were.

Fergus jumped into the void. "Trust me, we have no time to explain. Conall has been kidnapped by some very vengeful men who threatened to kill him. Your father is working with the Garda to bring him home. We'll take my car. OK?"

"My God, this is real," said JP.

"Very real," Fergus replied softly. "Here's a map of East Cork and the Naglas Mountains where Conall is being held in an old tower. It's more of a stable now. Your father took me on a practice drive yesterday so I would know where to turn and hide my car. Every minute counts now. The kidnappers could kill Conall before we get him out."

"But—" JP protested, flabbergasted. He looked at his mother for some reasonable explanation of this sudden implosion of his world.

Mary stood mute as she watched the men drive off, struggling with her own sense of terror that her peace-loving, anti-war husband who couldn't kill game-birds or deer, now seemed prepared to use an axe to save Conall, and perhaps Liam if necessary.

A sudden chill gripped her. *No, no,* she thought, arms now squeezed tightly across her breasts. *And with only an old, dull axe, Fergus You are, most definitely, not a knight of old, roaring off in some stupid crusade for the honor, for God and country. Men! This is not how families show love and respect. Or is it?*

Chapter Thirteen

Follow the pine trees

Several hours later, the rescue vehicles gathered just beyond a single lane road, northeast of Cork. Some still called it Park Avenue North. No one used it anymore – it was more of a path with no curbs, and only overgrown ditches. Just rows of recently planted pine trees, all of the same height and equal spacing.

Fergus and JP followed, and briefly caught sight of the ambulance from Cork. They edged closer, unsure of the ultimate location of the tower. All they knew was that the turnoff was just north of Power's Bridge, which was a small stone bridge over the trickle of water in the Bunaglanna River. Mercifully, there was no other traffic on the almost uninhabited road.

They saw a small bobbing light ahead marking the entrance of the side road and protected with only a small swinging bar. The chain and padlock had already been left dangling thanks to two hammer blows by the Garda.

"Quickly now," said Seamus quietly, "move your car down the road, and follow the tire tracks on the right between the second and third rows of pine trees. The reforestation is a blessing, with its bed of pine needles, so there will be no broken branches underfoot. I'll walk ahead and carry the light. Say a silent prayer until the rescue team smashes the tower door open. Anything else, Fergus, before we move out?"

"Just one thing, Seamus. Make sure there will be room on the road for the ambulance to turn around and rush to a Cork hospital. If Conall is still alive, Liam will be riding in the ambulance with him, and will call their mother at home. If, if…we're too late, Lord I pray not, Bishop Jack will be standing by at the home for final prayers…if…needed."

John Patrick, youngest member of the family and the most outraged, said between clenched teeth, "Beds of pine needles or whatever, will Uncle Conall know or even care? Nice and neat too. Bull Shit! Why would they take Uncle Conall? Whom did he ever hurt? Letting the Garda tell us what…"

"Enough!" Seamus mouthed back at him. "This is a crime scene and you're not even a lawyer yet. I don't have time to explain the difference. Got that? Every second we stand here puts your Uncle Conall at risk, not to mention the Garda officers and your father and. Fergus. Get this kid out of my way or I'll cuff him to a pine tree."

As they moved forward, Fergus led the way on foot, guided by only a small torch. He wondered pointlessly whether the Irish police would call its big truck a Paddy Wagon. *That's too awful,* he told himself. *Pay attention.*

A time for gas masks

Everyone had been well drilled in Job One priorities: crash through the front door, take out Conall's captors, dead or alive, and cut the detonator line on his vest before its lethal package exploded into his gut and killed him.

So much for theory.

Still in the dark shadows away from the moon, each team member put on his gas mask.

"Check the fit," Seamus told them. "We're using CS gas in canisters, as do most police forces around the world for crowd control and hostage incidents. It's named after the two men who devolved the formula back the late 20s.

"What's important to know, particularly in this case, is that we're dealing with much older men who may have respiratory or cardiac problems. And of course the victim, whom we're told was physically beaten when kidnapped. Let's assume he has not been well fed, and may be more dead than alive.

"The first priority is to get Mr. Fitzgerald out alive, and into the waiting ambulance for transport back to a Cork hospital. At the family's request, I have the primary responsibility for rescuing Conall, as I have met him in better circumstances.

"I am also carrying wire cutters for the detonator lead to the explosives packed around his waist. God and Saint Patrick save both of us. Liam will be with us to identify his brother Conall.

"You all know your assignments. Once inside, activate the CS aerosol canisters near each kidnapper. Spray them with CS to shock and confuse them, and then pull them outside into the night air where our medical people can check them for cardiac, eye and lung problems that are common in older people. Take notes, and get the names of each kidnapper. It's possible that one or two of them may not survive the trip back to Cork. They will each face serious charges. Any questions?"

"Just one sir. How do we get in?"

"By the front door. Fergus will knock it off its hinges with his axe, then Liam and I will kick it in. Until you hear it crash, stay hidden in the shadows.

"And remain silent," Seamus continued. "It's a round tower, about five hundred years old with a diameter of at least 20 metres. It has four narrow windows and a sharp smell of animal waste. The odor is a leftover from the old hay cover. There are no animals on the site.

"Unless Conall has been moved since the photos of him were released, he should be directly in front of the door at the far stone wall. We expect the four kidnappers will be sleeping two aside. So, the first two constables split to either side and immediately, I mean very immediately, you other two take the others. Same drill then: hit them with CS gas and quickly pull the gas masks over them. We want them alive, cuffed and breathing when you escort them into the open air for transport to Cork for interrogation and physical examination.

"Oh, I almost forgot, Liam Fitzgerald, the editor of *The Times*, has been riding with the ambulance. Once the kidnappers are under our control, he will be free to contact his family with news of Conall.

"Afterward, he will contact his newsroom, which has been silent on the kidnapping. Once his newsroom breaks the story, we're bound to start receiving calls from other outlets wanting details.

"Now gentlemen, take your places for the attack."

Chapter Fourteen

Squeaky door

An old man's bladder took priority when he opened the door from the inside, and stepped along the far side of the tower wall.

Fergus quietly laid his axe down on the ground near the wall.

Seamus signaled him to wait, not knowing whether other kidnappers would follow the old man out of the castle.

Seconds passed, feeling like hours, but none of the other kidnappers followed.

The crisis passed like free-flow urine, and Fergus crawled forward, a man on a mission with his axe at his side and heart pounding.

Whack! Whack! He easily released the old hinges. Then he rolled aside as Seamus and Liam rose out of the gloom, and hurriedly bashed in the ages-old, now sagging wooden door, allowing the other officers to rush by.

Only three of the four kidnappers were wild-eyed scared when the CS gas hit them. They were instantly disoriented, eyes stinging and lungs gasping until the gas masks were pulled over their heads. Before they could sort out what had happened, they were pulled into the night air and cuffed. The fourth kidnapper had to be carried out, arms hanging loosely at his side, and barely breathing. Nor could he be revived.

Liam was successful with his assignment. Conall was barely aware when Liam cut the detonator cord. He didn't seem to know what was happening or even to recognize his brother. But he was breathing, and it was Liam, the good brother, who shed tears.

Fergus cried a little too as he moved to help Liam lift Conall to his feet, and walk slowly out of the tower past the three captives who were struggling to stand steadily with their hands cuffed behind them. The Garda team hustled the old kidnappers into the Paddy Wagon. One started to yell, "It's not over. We'll be back—"

"It's over for him," said a young Garda officer, looking down at the corpse. "I think I know, err, knew him. He never had a chance."

Seamus came to his side. "Are you sure? How do you know him?"

"We were different generations, but from the same area, Tipperary. I recall his da was an early member of the Sinn Fein and, jasus, was executed by the British .There would have been great pressure on his son to avenge his father's death."

"Your da, was he a Feinian too?"

"Luckily, he became a teacher, and moved to Cork."

The End

Death in Safe Harbor

A short story by Jake Doherty

In the end, death came suddenly, at once brutally and ignominiously for Capt. Jonas Isaiah Adams. His flight to Canada ended in a small stone and wooden hut on the Bruce Peninsula along the West Shore of Ontario's Georgian Bay. No more wars, no medals, and, as a coroner would later conclude, just a deep injury from a blunt instrument in the back of his skull.

Only one person would see him die.

It was all about money, not valor or the New England ring to his name.

Of course, nobody knew who Jonas was when he was found face down with a bloody hole in the back of his skull.

He appeared to have been surprised from behind, then propelled forward by the blow, smashing the right lens in his glasses. Fragments from a broken coffee cup littered the wooden floor around one of his hands. Jonas, a tall white male in his 40s, was dressed all in black with heavy combat boots – well-worn though clean. Thick leather gloves were found in the right side pocket of his jacket, and a black balaclava, neatly folded, was in the left.

He was not wearing a wedding ring and the lobe on his left ear was missing. The scar was neat, indicating that the injury had been well and promptly attended to.

Members of the Boxing Day Bird Count expedition found him after they had snow shoed into the Cabot Head Provincial Nature Reserve north of Dyers Bay. As usual, they used the old cabin to warm up before heading home. Nellie Tannahill, from Wiarton, just south on Colpoys Bay, was the first to spot Adams. She let out a yelp that send her blood pressure rocketing.

"Grab her," said one of her fellow birders. Jean Laforet, a retired school principal, promptly gave Nellie a belt of the brandy he always carried on such outings, careful and well prepared birder that he was.

They both took another belt when a second body was found in a backroom, dead from a gunshot wound in his chest. He was dressed much the same as Jonas, except for a yellow rain jacket with a hood. And heavy green rubber boots with felt liners.

"Oh my gawd, look at them would ya," said Nellie as the brandy gave her courage to take a second look. She bent over, holding her red and white toque with a band of small maple leaves, and ran her other hand through her gray, tightly wound curls. "Like they just dropped from the sky or washed up, ending up here. And with winter setting in and all. Two dead ducks from the bird count, and nicely frozen at that."

Complications set in quickly. After several tries on a cell phone, one birder reached his wife at Lion's Head, midway up the Peninsula who, in turn, reached the Ontario Provincial Police detachment in Wiarton. The OPP quickly contacted officers checking snowmobile trails in the Cabot Head area and diverted them to the old cabin hidden in the evergreens and shore rocks circling Wingfield Basin.

At first sight, nothing was obvious except that the victims most likely had been dead for some time. That removed any suspicion that Nellie or her birder friends could possibly be suspects. Early winter storms had wiped out any tracks left by the killer – or killers for that matter. Nor did the deceased still have their wallets, which must have been removed by the killer.

Capt. Adams, however, still wore his military dog tags around his neck under a heavy turtleneck, unnoticed by the killer. Only one bag of clothing for two victims, a satchel with a small shaving kit, and only a little leftover food, barely enough to sustain them for two or three days.

"Most likely just passing through," said Corporal Mike Erskine to his patrol buddy, Rob Exner. As young patrol officers, neither had any homicide experience. Clearly though, the circumstances of the two deaths suggested foul play, and not suicides or natural causes.

"Why here?" said Rob, putting aside his snowmobile helmet.

"Who knows?" said Mike, "Let's just declare this a crime scene, secure the area, and call for help from Wiarton. Back to basics, rookie. Get every ones' name and then organize a quick check of the area. We'll lose daylight in a couple of hours. Maybe, just maybe, there are more bodies out there."

Erskine stayed behind while Exner moved into the flock of birders, who were all anxious to leave, except Nellie, of course, who was looking for a cell phone to call the *Sun Times* in Owen Sound.

"I'm the correspondent here, and these are my mur---well my story, and I gots a job to do, so I stay, eh?"

"Okay, stay then, but don't touch anything. Just look—and find some coffee, if you can."

Erskine was much more interested in the dog tags under the victim's sweater. The tag revealed his last name, his service number and blood type.

"So that's who you are…J.I. Adams from God knows where…and no clue how you got here."

The second body had no tags, but displayed some nasty scars on the left shoulder.

"One of our boys, eh?" asked Nellie looking over Mike's shoulder. "Better call the Meaford Military base, they'll know."

"Madam," said Erskine brusqly, "please stand back—"

"Just Nellie please. OK, call the tank range. My husband used to work there, and…here's the number."

"Nellie, go find the coffee!"

"Just trying to help you fine fellas. OPP and all. No reason to get pushy."

"Whatever, Nellie."

Social niceties over, Erskine made the call to the Wiarton detachment, which, in turn, called CFB Meaford with the information. The answer came back quickly.

"So Corporal, who's our man Adams?"

"It appears," said Erskine checking his notes, "that Mr. Adams is not even one of ours."

"Not an enlisted man or vet?" said Nellie, who was listening in on one side of the conversation. "Not even our military? Are we at war? What sort of wacko was the late Mr. Adams?"

"Easy Nellie, don't jump to conclusions. A Meaford official suggested we try the U.S. military. It uses a different tag system."

Constable Exner had other priorities. A lanky man from northern Alberta who had come east when his banker father was transferred to Owen Sound, Exner had lived in the Bruce long enough to respect squall weather in winter. Offshore winds were already picking up. Roads would close, schools would shut down in the morning when nothing could move in the blinding blur of wind-whipped snow.

Even on a crime scene.

"If you'll pardon an old woman, Constable, sir," said Nellie, hands on her ample hips, looking out the window, "them bodies aren't moving out of here tonight. There's no hurry for the coroner now, so let's divide my gang into two groups."

"Nellie, this is police business. I wish you would find some coffee as Mike."

By now Exner had begun to let his frustration show.

"Mike, er, Corporal," another birder interjected, "a couple of quick suggestions if I—"

"You too?" said Erskine, looking at the anxious faces watching him. He was experienced enough to take advice, though not always easily. "Shoot, quick-like!"

Exner quickly surveyed the birders' reactions, and stepped into the center of the room.

"First," he said, "does anyone have a camera or a cell phone? Over there? Right on. If you would sir, take several shots of the bodies as they are now. The crime scene guys won't be here, perhaps until morning, and we should move the bodies into the back room and cover them. I think I saw a tarp in there Two helpers over there? Good. The rest of us can stay here."

Nellie, never shy, intervened. "I got a marker pen in me purse. Can I trace the outline of the bodies first? That's what they do on TV."

"Get to it then," said Corporal Erskine, stepping forward to regain control. "Now Nellie, I need a small group of volunteers with heavy snow boots and jackets, well folks who can divide the perimeter, and move out for a hundred meters or so, within sight of the cabin. We can't make assumptions there are only these two bodies. There may be more. If anyone out there needs help, just holler."

"Like this, HELP, HELP," Nellie blasted, full force into everyone's face," and just keep yelling HELP."

"Ooh Nellie, that's a bit loud. Oh, madam, yes you in the back, you've found candles? Great."

Within minutes, the birders had organized themselves into a radial search. Most had flashlights of their own, stomping around with walking sticks. The two officers positioned themselves at the front and back of the cabin. There was no chatter at first, just the roar of the waves pounding ashore from Georgian Bay, and the first rush of squall weather through the trees.

Except for Nellie, who charged head down, hands shielding her eyes until she bounced off a big rock and then into a tree. "I need help. No, not that kind of help. Art, just lift me up."

Their giggling stopped abruptly.

"Over here," said a voice about five meters to the left of them at the shoreline. "HELP, HELP. I've found a boat. HELP, HELP."

As had Sherry Wilkie from the Mar hamlet on Highway 6. She stood beside an old fishing boat, high and dry out of the water, long and low with high plywood sides.

Erskine reached her first. He looked inside the boat. Nothing.

"At least we know where it's from," said Sherry, cleaning snow off her glasses to read the faint lettering on the stern: "From Upper Michigan. And its name…let me take a closer look…Mekong Delta? What's that? Chinese?"

"No," said Nellie catching up. "Vietnamese. Me nephew died there."

No one slept easily that night, scrunched together as they were, with no blankets and only packsacks under their heads. Three of the four cell phones brought by the birders were now dead.

As dawn began to break about 7 am, Nellie recognized the place where the boat had been found – a small safe harbor just north of the Cabot Head Light, marked on most navigation maps for small craft caught in strong easterly winds across Georgian Bay. Buoys marked the entrance, but the channel, though narrow, was passable. Barely.

She found the two officers looking out a window facing the water.

"Wind's easing," said Mike. "We may get help soon." Turning to Exner, he added, "So what do we report? We know one victim's name, the name of the boat and where it came from. But we don't know why the victims challenged the weather across Lake Huron to get here from Michigan."

As usual, Nellie couldn't help herself.

"Not so," she said, holding up her cell phone. "I had one bar left so I called back to the *Sun Times*. News of a good murder travels fast. Folks wanna know."

Erskine responded quickly, trying not to show that he had been caught off guard. "We'll hold a media briefing as planned when the coroner arrives with the crime scene guys, and we can get you civilians safely home."

"Civilians?" snorted Nellie. "So youse don't want to know what I got? Or do I hold my own police briefing?"

Exner interjected. "Mike, err sir, perhaps we might take a preliminary report from Nellie."

Erskine nodded his approval.

"Well folks," said Nellie, facing her birder friends. "The *Sun Times* passed my first report yesterday to *QMI*, our Sun Media wire service in Toronto. And when the Yank angle was spotted, *Canadian Press* eventually passed it along to *Associated Press* in New York and Washington, where calls were made. Everyone in Owen Sound knows about it now."

"Not me," piped Jean Laforet, now standing beside her. "So, whattya know?"

"Okay, then. The late Jonas Isaiah Adams was a captain in the Michigan National Guard who had already, it seems, served two tours – one in Iraq and the other in Afghanistan. Bunch of medals. But Jonas had been called for a third tour even though he was engaged in big fights with Veterans Affairs. His family doc believed he suffered from post-traumatic stress and was not fit for active duty.

"You mean PTSD?" offered George.

"Ya, that's it. Nightmares, strange behavior and depressions. High suicide rate for these guys. But the VA said no, and he still had to go. Then his wife left him when he began writing anti-war letters to the local newspaper there."

"Sounds like the Vietnam War," said Jean, "when I came to Canada through the tunnel at Windsor. Made a good life here. But not now though. I read a newspaper item recently that deserters will now be treated like criminals, and I guess, sent back to the United States for whatever the U.S. Military wants to do with them. No safe harbor here anymore."

Distant sounds of approaching snowmobiles and a plow brightened spirits around the room, and all the birders gathered around the windows. "Hope they have warm coffee," said one. A woman wanted tea. "And decaffeinated, please."

The two officers went outside. "So Rob, it seems probable that Adams was sneaking into Canada the hard way. And lost the gamble."

"But we don't know who else was with them, or who was waiting here for them. There's another person out there, probably alive."

Within minutes of the OPP arrival on a gloriously bright December day, the coroner pronounced that Captain Jonas Adams and his friend has been dead for five or six weeks and that death for one was probably caused by a blow to the head with a blunt weapon and gunshot to the chest of the other. Autopsies would be needed to confirm the initial findings. As soon as the bodies were tagged and bagged and taken out to the road on a snowmobile sled, everyone began to relax with coffee and trailmix bars. And lots of hugs among the birding groups, some of whom were in tears.

Sherry Wilkie broke away from her fellow birders to take in the strange beauty and quietness of Wingfield Basin, and the irony of death in a safe harbor. She pushed a small drift of snow on some beach rocks to secure better footing, and looked down.

A small tab of black material sticking out of the snow near her feet grabbed her attention. Just one big hole in it, no, no, maybe more she thought and pulled it out.

"YO…" she cried, but then remembered the signal. "HELP, HELP. I've found something." Nellie Tannahill and Corporal Erskine were quickly at her side.

"Oh my gosh," said Nellie. "It's a…a—"

"Another balaclava," added Erskine, pushing the two women aside. Quickly, he called out to his patrol mate who found an evidence bag in his parka. "We'll need the forensics lab in Toronto to check these because we now have three balaclavas and two corpses."

And with that, the birding group and the police made their way back to the Cabot Head Light House and their own cars and vans. The road was now open, and they were anxious to resume the Christmas Week they would never forget. They even posed for a group shot for the *Sun Times* and the *Wiarton Echo*.

Two weeks later, after the New Year, the OPP finally held a media conference in the detachment headquarters just south of Wiarton. – a big event in a small town.

"What about the third balaclava?" yelled Nellie.

"Yeah," followed Sherry. "We found it, so what's it mean, whose is it, you know what I mean?"

Erskine tugged at his collar. "You're right of course. I should have referred to it sooner. Nothing conclusive, no charges have been laid, but the forensics team traced the salvia on the inside of the third balaclava – we must withhold the name for the moment – to an older Vietnam veteran now living in Ontario. What we don't know is whether he also took in refugees. Had he arranged to meet the victims there, only to be caught in a storm? What was his role?

"The second victim was also from Upper Michigan, and owned the boat. At this point we can only speculate the motive was robbery. The U.S. investigators told us that Capt. Adams had withdrawn substantial amounts of money from his bank account in November, presumably to start a new life here. If so, where is that money now?"

Then Erskine stood silent for a moment. "Had Capt. Adams survived the trip, he would have been deported back to the U.S., and, we understand, received treatment in a Veterans' Hospital for his depression. His case was already under review when he left Michigan. Unfortunately, he did not know that his third tour of duty was about to be cancelled. Rob, care to add to that?"

"What a waste of a good man."

The End

Acknowledgments

Let me first explain my gratitude for what follows, and, most particularly, how they moved the plot points along, and shaped my thinking about kidnapping in Ireland, and the underlying theme of inter-generational revenge.

This is the "why" question about Ireland: will the Republic of Ireland, now prosperous and proud, move firmly beyond the old hatreds that warped many of their children?

* A Social Policy Report About Children and Terrorism, written by by four researchers at Loyola University in Chicago: James Gabbarino, Amy Governale, Patrick Henry, and Danielle Nesi.

*Much credit goes to the Garda, Ireland's national and local police force, comparable to Canada's RCMP and provincial forces like the Ontario Provincial Police. While the Garda's own regulations prohibit the sharing of its own tactical procedures about kidnapping, we did find a way to affirm the use of CS gas used to neutralize the kidnappers, and safely extracting a potential victim.

*Son Michael Liam Doherty of Burlington, On., a planner by profession, used his research skills and curiosity to identify which of Cork's many tower castles would be used by the kidnappers to hold their victim, and what rarely-used roads could be used without notice.

My other three children – Denise, Francoise and Conall. were sharp-eyed readers.

*Our own base camp was the River Lee Hotel where several of its staff gathered a collection of Irish slang words that helped bring to life the Canadian prose about another culture.

*My local editor in Owen Sound, Ann Findley Stewart, was my first reader. Her web page – owensoundhub.org -- had published one of my short stories in serial form – "Death in Safe Harbor" – that was well received, and that later appeared in print.

*Much credit and wisdom was again provided by Donna Carrick of Carrick Publishing, a fine writer herself and a general, all around miracle worker.

*It's my own Irish blood that took me to Cork, warm and generous people that they are. "Oh, you're from Canada, are you? Let me pay for this." Which they often did.

JAKE DOHERTY

About the Author

The writing challenges faced by Jake Doherty these days are his two thumbs, particularly the big knuckles on each hand. They tend to miss the space bar too often, now that arthritis has settled in.

Other than that, his writing is still exploring new styles and he's very excited about using his subconscious more often in his work. Solutions come more easily, now that he prefers to write in the morning after a good sleep. A neurologist friend explained that the brain at rest engages about 70 per cent of itself, far more and faster than the day shift.

Jake now lives in Acton, Ontario. His email address is johnjakedoherty@gmail.com and his telephone number is (519) 853-0636.

What's next?

His four children and 11 grandchildren want him to write an autobiography about his much-travelled life as a journalist for 40 years. His late wife Monique often raised the same idea.

Hmm...

JAKE DOHERTY

REVENGE IS A FAMILY AFFAIR

JAKE DOHERTY

www.ingramcontent.com/pod-product-compliance
Lightning Source LLC
Chambersburg PA
CBHW022044170626
46808CB00003B/1364